"My Friend Punker"

Is written and illustrated
by April Barry

Copyright © 2002
April Barry, All rights reserved
Printed in the United Kingdom
First Edition October 2002

ISBN: 0-9539722-3-2

www.thecatland chronicles

also by the Author:
'A Twelfth Night Tale'
'The Birthday'

Published by Mercia Image Limited

My friend

PUNKER.

This is a true story.

for

Beryl.

by

April Barry.

'My Friend Punker'
is
Beryl's story.

Beryl used to live near me. She was already an old lady in 1990, when she told me the story of her cat Punker, in a few brief sentences. I asked Beryl if she would allow me to write her story. Permission was granted. Beryl is of course the little girl in the story. I have changed her name to Isabel.

This is for Beryl.

The Brave.

Fine smooth cheeked boys, bright faced,
Some straight from school,
Rushed to enlist, adding years,
Thus foiling the rule.
In dank trenches they sheltered
In deep mud so cold.
Over the top they went, most died
No chance to grow old.

Husbands and sweethearts,
Uncles, fathers, brothers,
Bravely sacrificed themselves,
Dying for others.
Though almost nine decades
Have passed since then,
They fought for us now,
Those valiant men.

In Memory of

All the Brave Men who died in action during the 1914-1918 War, and also dedicated to those who survived, none of whom came home totally unscathed.

Remembering too those who served and died in later wars.

In Memory of
the Brave Cavalry Horses
who died while serving so faithfully in the 1914-1918 war.

During the early months of the War, the Cavalry played a worthy part, but by October 1914 there was no role for them on the Western Front. They still played a great part in Palestine and Mesopotamia (now Iraq), and also on the Eastern Front.

From the outset, armoured cars were used to augment the Cavalry. Tanks began to replace them in 1916.

In loving memory of Cavalry Officer Jacek Lopuszanski's splendid horse
MAX.

Cavalry Officer J. Lopuszanski with his horse MAX.

In Memory of
the Brave War Dogs
who died while serving so
faithfully in the 1914-1918 war.

A war dog school was established
at Shoeburyness in Essex, and the
dogs were trained for sentry duties,
as message carriers, to lay telephone
lines and to carry ammunition. The
trained dogs proved extremely useful.
    The dogs that were most suitable
and easy to train for war work
were German Shepherds, collies,
labradors and lurchers.

Labrador Retriever.

German Shepherd
or Alsatian.

Lurcher.

Collie.

Hello children. I am a very old lady now, and my name is Isabel. I live all by myself in a little house with a brown front door.

Nowadays I use a walking stick to lean on when I go shopping, and I walk very slowly, with faltering steps.

However, once upon a time, long years ago, I was young and spritely, just like you; running and skipping about, and playing exciting games.

Oh yes, those were indeed such happy days.

I wonder if you have ever heard of the First World War? Well it took place between the years 1914 - 1918.

Everyone thought that it would be the war to end all wars. Unfortunately they were very wrong.

At that time I was a little imp; a schoolgirl of eight years old. Now I would like to tell you a story about something good which happened to me during those War Years.

At least, that is if you have time to listen.

In spite of the war, home life con--tinued almost as usual for me, except for the fact that my big brother Henry had to become a soldier.

He, and many other young men like him, had to go away to fight in the war. We were all so very proud of Henry.

Mama had insisted that he should have his photograph taken wearing his uniform, and now he gazed at us all every day, from his place of honour on the piano.

I missed him badly, but my parents were at home, and so I felt secure.

In those days, I didn't like cats at all. In fact I remember that I was rather afraid of them. Mama endeavoured many times to help me to overcome my fear, but in vain.

One afternoon, it was a Monday I remember, I returned happily to school as usual, not thinking for one moment that something most important would happen that day.

However, it did, I am happy to say.

In school I sat next to a girl called Ruby. She was a mischievous girl, who was always laughing and playing pranks, but I liked her.

The afternoon passed slowly by. Some of us drifted into drowsy day dreams, lulled by the buzzing of a fat bumble bee knocking against the window pane. The smell of chalk dust and polish lingered in the warm school room air.

I noticed that during the afternoon, Ruby kept opening her desk lid to peep quickly inside.

I thought that I could hear squeaks and scuffles coming from the interior. I was soon to find out the reason for this. When Miss Rose rang the bell to announce the end of afternoon school, we packed away our books quietly, and stood behind our chairs to sing the after-noon hymn. After wishing Miss Rose "Good Afternoon," we were allowed to leave.

Happily I followed Ruby from the playground, hoping that we might walk home together. All of a sudden she turned to me, and laughingly asked, "Do you want this Isabel?"

12.

Before I could reply, she swiftly pushed something warm into the front of my pinafore. Then away she sped, while I stood rooted to the spot.

Then suddenly something moved against my blouse, and I felt extremely frightened. I ran home as fast as my black stockinged legs would carry me. My long hair streamed on the wind.

Thankfully I reached home, and flung myself through the back door, and into the kitchen where Mama was waiting for me.

"Mama, Mama," I cried, "Ruby has put something inside my pinafore. Whereupon I dashed tearfully into her arms.

Mama quickly investigated. Now what do you think she took out of my pinafore? You will be surprised to hear that it was a tiny black kitten.

"Oh, the poor, dear little thing!" exclaimed Mama. "I must give him some milk." Which she did.

When he was lapping noisily, she comforted me, and tried to encourage me to approach the kitten, but I just couldn't. I felt afraid of him, even though he was so small and friendly.

There was great excitement in our household, for at the weekend, my big brother Henry was to come home on leave.

It was Monday when the kitten arrived. Mama took great care of him, and constantly attempted to help me to overcome my fear of him, for that was her way.

I gradually became used to him, as I watched him greedily lapping milk from his special blue saucer, or playing with a paper ball, suspended on some string, which Mama had made for him.

No one gave him a name. He was simply known as The Kitten. Somehow I began to be fascinated by him, and I looked forward to seeing his cheerful little face, each morning before my departure for school, and each evening on my return.

I began to enjoy watching his playful antics in the house, and outside in the garden. I even ventured to play games like hide and seek with him, but I was still far too timid to touch him.

20.

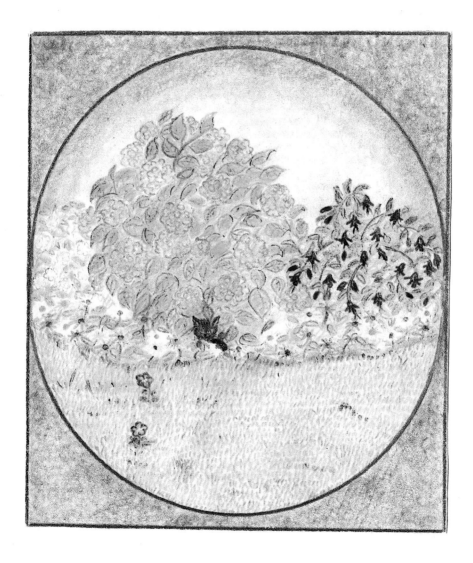

I was sitting on my own comfortable little chair, half listening to Papa's kind voice droning on and on, and half dreaming of my big brother Henry, my Hero, who was soon to arrive.

Suddenly my pleasant reverie was interrupted, and I felt a small body climb onto my knee. My hand touched warm, soft fur, and I heard a loud purring sound. The kitten had decided that if I wouldn't make friends with him, then he would have to do some-thing about it. I am so very glad that he did.

24.

He crouched there, gazing up at me with his luminous, lovely eyes. It seemed to me that he was half expecting to be rejected. My fear simply vanished. A feeling of tenderness overwhelmed me, and I began to stroke the tiny creature, whereupon he began to knead me with his tiny paws. He was purring ecstatically meanwhile. Eventually he curled up as close to me as he could.

Mama smiled gently, for she was truly pleased. I sat there with him until bedtime, and from that night onwards, we became firm friends.

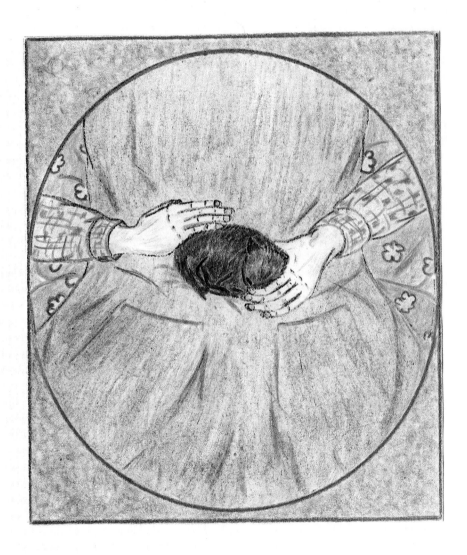

Well children, that is not quite the end of my story. Remember that my kitten didn't have a name. You can per-haps guess who decided what to call him. Yes, you're quite right; it was my big brother Henry.

He arrived amidst a flurry of hug-ging and talking. It was a happy day. Sometime later, I was sitting with the kitten on my knee, when my brother exclaimed, "Why, Isabel, your kitten looks exactly like Punker! Let's call him Punker." So of course, we did. I should imagine that he was the only kitten in England to be named after a President.

My brother explained to me that the French President's name was really Monsieur Raymond Poincaré, however he and his soldier comrades preferred to call him Punker.

My little kitten Punker grew into a fine, handsome cat, and he lived happily with us for many, many years.

Since that day so long ago, when he first climbed onto my knee in friendship, I have never been afraid of cats again.

I will always remember my friend Punker with love and gratitude.

Scarlet Poppies.

The scarlet poppies gently blow,
Frail petals fluttering
'Neath Summer skies.
Long gone
Are the dreadful killing fields.
Beauty lives,
Where once gallant soldiers died.

Scarlet poppies blow for short lived lives,
For lost hopes and dreams,
For sharp agony and pain.
But scarlet poppies bloom
In burgeoning hope,
All those brave soldiers
Did not die in vain.

For each life lost a scarlet poppy grows.
The Fallen
Will thus be remembered for ever.
Eternally
The soldiers' red flower blows,
A flower for each soul.
Will we forget? NEVER!